MANCHESTER

Edited By Megan Roberts

First published in Great Britain in 2019 by:

 Young**Writers**

Young Writers
Remus House
Coltsfoot Drive
Peterborough
PE2 9BF
Telephone: 01733 890066
Website: www.youngwriters.co.uk

FOREWORD

Welcome, Reader!

Here at Young Writers our aim is to encourage creativity in children and to inspire a love of the written word. Each competition we create is tailored to the relevant age group, hopefully giving each child the inspiration and incentive to create their own piece of work, whether it's a poem or a short story. We truly believe that seeing their work in print gives pupils a sense of achievement and pride.

For Young Writers' latest nationwide competition, Spooky Sagas, we gave primary school pupils the task of tackling one of the oldest story-telling traditions: the ghost story. However, we added a twist – they had to write it as a mini saga, a story in just 100 words!

These pupils rose to the challenge magnificently and this resulting collection of spooky sagas will certainly give you the creeps! You may meet friendly ghosts or creepy clowns, or be taken on Halloween adventures to haunted mansions and ghostly graveyards!

So if you think you're ready... read on.

CONTENTS

Ricardo Singh (10) 57
Doyin Adedeji (10) 58
Jake Cutler (11) 59
Ruby Davies (10) 60
Lewis Arthur Thompson (10) 61
Umer Nadeem (11) 62
Daniyal Khan (10) 63
Isabel Hope Nichols (11) 64
Fateenah Eniola Soneye (11) 65
Skye Tyson (11) 66
Musa Waqas (10) 67
Ricardas Balciunas (11) 68
Thomas Jackson (11) 69
Abdullah Omar Shawish (10) 70
Mason Lewis (10) 71

St Anthony's Catholic Primary School, Wythenshawe

Irene Momoh (10) 72
Stephan Kurian (8) 73
Scarlett Cork (9) 74
Katie Elorm Mensah (9) 75
Kioni Hannaway (7) 76
Sandra Wlodarczyk (9) 77
Panashe Musungwa (10) 78
Olivia Mulvey (10) 79
Alfie Hackney (7) 80
Takudaishe Musungua (7) 81
Rosie McMahon (8) 82
Mateusz Steczkiewicz (10) 83
Amira Lydia Brew-Butler (9) 84
Lord Michael Ojage (8) 85
Mahimsa Gallenahene 86
Mohottala (8)
Rodrigo Mendes (9) 87
Alicia Louise Jasmine Tyler (7) 88
Sofia Evangeline Daniel (9) 89
Ahad Khan (10) 90

St Barnabas CE Primary Academy, Manchester

Eunice Kipila Moungala (10) 91
Olivia Louise Donaldson (11) 92
Emmanuella Esther 93
Anazodo (11)
Cordell Stratton (10) 94
Skye Sharkey (10) 95
Brandon Corcoran (11) 96
Jorja Burns (10) 97
Aiden Gettings (10) 98
David James (10) 99
Amna Ahmed (11) 100
Destiny Tamia Knight (10) 101

St John's CE Primary School, Failsworth

Elliott Andrew Backhouse (10) 102
Lilly Crumlish (10) 103
Oliver Duff (9) 104
Adriarna Coley (9) 105
Luke Hulme (10) 106
William Barker (10) 107
Lillie-Mae Nuttall (11) 108
Emmie Coyne (10) 109
Max Graham (10) 110
Megan Eaton (10) 111
Maisy Moe McCaffery (10) 112
Ben Burgess (9) 113
Ruby Towers (10) 114
Pawlo Capewell (11) 115
Abbey Farmer (11) 116
Ferne Bate (9) 117
Dylan Barrett (11) 118
Laila Kesgin (10) 119
Brooke Leigh Flynn (10) 120
Ryan Brandon Osbaldeston (9) 121
Sophie Bradley (10) 122
Nico Wrigley (10) 123
George-Christopher Brooks (10) 124
Emily Dunn (9) 125
Lexi Simpson (10) 126

THE
SPOOKY
SAGAS

SHADOWS OF DARKNESS

I crept into the forbidden attic. Suddenly, the door shut. Things mysteriously started to move, zooming past me. The moonlight revealed a figure like a vampire! I attempted to escape but my legs felt shaky as I fell and fainted for what seemed like an hour. Then I woke to find myself lying on the floor as a sinister figure stared wide-eyed into my eyes, looming over me. I tried to get up but couldn't. I looked towards the person's face to see my sister. "Got you!" she shouted, laughing. "Let's go," I suggested in relief.

Alzahraa Nagi Ali (9)
Cravenwood Primary Academy, Crumpsall

MY ENCOUNTER OF THE TIKWI

One long, winter afternoon, I was walking home from a tiresome workday when suddenly, I was stopped dead in my tracks. A dreadful noise filled my ears, it was unbearable and I thought I'd heard it before. It was the sound of the Tikwi! It got closer, saying, "Tikwi!"
Did I just hear a Tikwi? A Tikwi was a demon that separated from its body every night to hunt for fresh blood. I ran for the bus and I was relieved because the noise got further away. That night, I had encountered and run away from the menacing Tikwi...

Mamsi Kumer (11)
Cravenwood Primary Academy, Crumpsall

THE HAUNTED HOUSE

I think my house is haunted. Sometimes I hear scary noises, were the noises from ghosts or witches or was it just my sisters? I think my house is haunted, the floorboards are always creaking. I think there's someone here, but it might be the mice running under the floorboards. I think my house is haunted, I hear howling noises in the night. It might be the old windows in my house that are falling apart. I think my house is haunted, I hear crying voices. They might be from dead people or the crying is from next door.

Zaiina Habib (8)
Cravenwood Primary Academy, Crumpsall

THE SPOOKY THING

I went shopping and found out that I was lost at night. It was dark and I was in a spooky place. I tried to get out and something came towards me. It was a shadow coming closer and closer... I started to walk backwards, I was terrified so I started to scream so loud that it came faster towards me. I was trapped and I thought it was the end for me, but it was not. It was only my friend, Tiffany! She'd been looking for me all that time! We went back home happily.

Saja Amiri (9)
Cravenwood Primary Academy, Crumpsall

BOBBY'S NEW FRIENDS

There was once a boy called Bobby. He was taking a walk until he bumped into a monsterific mansion. Obviously, Bobby went in because he was nosy. He felt he was being followed and he was. "Boo!" shouted Frank and Louise.

Bobby was amazed at this combination of monsters that he nearly fainted! "Why aren't you scared?" asked Louise.

"Because," Bobby said, "you're cool."

They couldn't believe their big, monstery ears.

"Really?" asked Frank, "No one's ever called us cool before."

"Well, I just did. Let's be friends!"

They were all well, they did everything together for the next year.

Megan Bennett (9)
Greswell Primary School & Nursery, Denton

WHAT A NIGHTMARE

The funeral day had arrived. James jumped out of bed, quickly got dressed and ran downstairs. His parents were dressed in black. Sat in the back of the funeral car, James was certain he could hear his gran's voice crying, "Help me!" Arriving at the church, the voice seemed to stop. As the coffin was lowered, James heard the voice again. He leaned forward, falling into the grave. He could feel hands grabbing his ankles, pulling him underground. "No!" James shouted. "Let me go!"

Just then, James' mum walked in, pulled off his duvet and said, "Time for school, James."

Calum Brown (9)
Greswell Primary School & Nursery, Denton

HARRY WAS HAVING A TERRIBLE NIGHTMARE

In Harry's room, he was sleeping when, unbelievably, he was woken up by a loud noise. "What was that noise?" he asked.
Well, that loud noise was a skeleton's bones crackling. Two minutes later, a hand made out of bones appeared from under Harry's bed! He decided to touch it and he started to turn into a skeleton!
But, he woke up once again. "Was it a nightmare?" Harry said.
"Yes, that one was, but this one isn't..." He was shocked, a hand came from behind the painting. "Oh no! There's a zombie in my wall! Argh!"

Oliver Jack Curran (9)
Greswell Primary School & Nursery, Denton

A GHOST IN THE CAR

A young girl in a pretty, white dress, holding a purse, flags down an old man for a ride. He gives her a ride to her great-grandmother's house. They talk about the old days. He drops her off.

The following day, when he gets into the car, he notices the purse was left behind. He drives to the great-grandmother's house with the purse. Her great-grandmother answers the door. He explains why he's there.

"I'm sorry sir, you have the wrong address. My great-granddaughter died many years ago wearing her favourite white dress after a night out dancing..."

Liam Armstrong (10)
Greswell Primary School & Nursery, Denton

TALES FROM THE OTHER SIDE

Finally, the night of our camping trip had arrived. My friend and I could feel the terror creeping up our spines, but the excitement engaged us. "What was that?" we screeched. Suddenly, we heard a muffled groaning and then snorting and snuffling. Was this the tormented soul of a dead soldier who fought in past battles? We were frozen in fear like a deer in the headlights. The tent started to shake, something was trying to get inside. "Argh! Go away! Leave us alone!" we screamed in fear. We ripped open the tent door and there stood a large cow!

Lucy Freeman (10)
Greswell Primary School & Nursery, Denton

SPIDERS

A spider ran across the forehead of a fifteen-year-old girl, who went by the name of Delaney. She was sleeping, small snores escaping her mouth. The spider paused, then carried on.

The next day, Delaney woke to an itchy forehead. It was like that all through school and she told her mother it was bothering her when she got home. Her mum just sighed and said, "It's probably nothing."

When she was showering the bump had grown to an incredibly large size. She itched it, the hot water burning her skin. Then, spiders exploded out of the wound!

William Pattinson (9)
Greswell Primary School & Nursery, Denton

THE MAZE OF FORBIDDEN HORROR

It was a gloomy evening, Jeff, Jim and Jill were playing and found a maze. They went in. Two ghosts came from nowhere and chased them deeper into the maze. Then a dozen skeletons came from the ground and forced them to go deeper into the maze. "This is all your fault Jeff!" exclaimed Jim.

"Yes, you're the one all brave and courageous!" said Jim.

"Stop arguing," exclaimed Jill, so they did.

Finally, they came to the centre. There lay a button. Jeff pressed it and all three of them were released, safe and sound.

George Mayson-Crashley (10)
Greswell Primary School & Nursery, Denton

SPOOKY STORIES

One dark and stormy night, Rachel was home alone as her parents had abandoned her so she went to sleep. Suddenly, her bedroom door locked. She jumped out of her bed and cried for help. Nobody answered. Then she saw a shadow lurking in the shadows. Her palms were sweaty and her heart was heavy. "Who are you?" she asked.

"I'm your worst nightmare!" they said as they tried to throw a punch. She took off his mask, she was shocked at who had tried to hurt her. It couldn't be!

"Uncle Fred?" Rachel said, confused...

Shalom Ofori (10)
Greswell Primary School & Nursery, Denton

MY FRIEND JEFF

I'm looking for my friend, Jeff, and there's only one place left to look: the basement. I hate the basement, it's dark and gloomy and very spooky. As I walk down the creaky stairs, into the dusty, old room, I see a figure in the distance. I shout out, "Jeff, are you there?" The figure lumbers forward. I step back in fright. "Where's Jeff? What have you done with him?"
As I flick on the dim light, I begin to scream as a vampire appears. "You looking for me?" Jeff says, wearing his Halloween costume.

Dylan Horsecroft (10)
Greswell Primary School & Nursery, Denton

THE HAUNTING STORY

On a horrible, foggy night, there were five children telling terrifying stories to each other. They were having lots of fun until one of the stories came true! There was a ghost haunting them, fog everywhere.

Through the week, there were even more clues, like claw marks and spooky words written in blood. Then, because of this, they set up cameras all around the building.

The next day, they saw a faint, ghost-like figure when they looked at the cameras. At this point, they were so scared. Three of them said it was all just a big joke.

Harry Highcock (10)
Greswell Primary School & Nursery, Denton

THE DEAD DREAM

Susan and Dave were graverobbers. Their shifts were done and they could now go home. They both had to go through the cemetery to get home but, suddenly, Dave heard a strange noise coming from the bushes. "Over there." Dave took a closer look and... There was a dead zombie! "Quick, we have to get out of here!"
They both rushed past the gates onto the road and back to their house. "We're never going there again," Susan said.
For a moment, Dave stopped. "Wait! Could this be a dream...?"

Suraya Wellington (9)
Greswell Primary School & Nursery, Denton

THE HAUNTED HOUSE

It was so scary walking towards the haunted house that everyone was gossiping about. In the distance, there were a plethora of graves outside the house. The trees brushed furiously along my neck. Trying to open the door, I fell in and the door slammed shut behind me. The floor creaked as I walked toward the living room. On the wall, there was a picture of Frankenstein. I started to walk upstairs and I heard whispering voices. "Hello? Is anyone there?"
I turned around. Mortifyingly, Fred jumped out! "You scared me!"

Ria Turner Groves (9)
Greswell Primary School & Nursery, Denton

THE ZOMBIE IN THE CELLAR

There once lived two very curious boys. They were excited one day as they were going to venture into the old, abandoned house next door which was boarded up. Once they were inside, they had to put dust masks on because it was so dusty. The pictures on the walls sent chills down their spines. After a lot of moving cobwebs, they found a damp cellar. Inside, they saw a mysterious figure in the darkness. It smelled horrible. As it moved closer and closer, the stench got stronger and stronger. It moved a little closer... It was a rotten zombie!

Finnlay Goulding (9)
Greswell Primary School & Nursery, Denton

THURSDAY THE 19TH

One dark, scary morning, my brother and I woke up in a witch's cauldron. The witch was getting ready to boil me and my brother! "I'm scared to my bones," said Jeff.

The mean, disgusting witch was planning to starve us. "I'm planning to starve you little horrors," said the witch.

Suddenly, the witch decided she wanted them fat but Jeff smartly found an exit and broke out. But, what would he do about me? I would have to stay because he was getting really far away from the old, wicked hag.

Steven Lamb (9)
Greswell Primary School & Nursery, Denton

TRUTH OR DARE?

It was Halloween night and a teenage girl was with her friends, playing truth or dare. At the end of the road, there was a haunted house. Her friends dared her to go in. Millie was really scared, but she wasn't chipping out of her dare. The first time she went in, she heard a noise from upstairs like someone was moving or stomping about. Millie started to walk up the squeaky stairs and saw a ghost! "I've got you!" Millie ran out of the house and she was never going in there again, well, not on her own.

Millie Lea Walker (9)
Greswell Primary School & Nursery, Denton

THE HOTEL

Once upon a time, Mr and Mrs Spooky and their dog, Crumbles, went on a trip to the haunted house where they were staying for the weekend. On arrival, they met Mr Bones, the hotel manager, who took them to their scary room. During the night, they woke up to a mysterious noise. *Tap! Tap! Tap!* went the noise. Mrs Spooky screamed out loud, which made Mr Spooky fall out of his bed. They found Crumbles under his bed, to his amazement, it was only Crumbles with wrapping paper! "Silly Crumbles!"

Holly Turner (10)
Greswell Primary School & Nursery, Denton

THE HOSPITAL

Once upon a time, there was a sister and a brother who went exploring to an abandoned hospital. But, to their surprise, nobody was there and they began to get scared. They looked around to find a dark room which had a strange, talking noise coming from it. That was the room where all of the dead people were. As they went to turn back, a male figure started to approach them, so they ran for their lives. Somehow, the dead man managed to trap them and double himself, so there were two dead men chasing them.

Ella Blossom Calvert (9)
Greswell Primary School & Nursery, Denton

ZOMBIE IN THE WARDROBE

One morning, a little boy called Alex had to do a dare. That dare was to go to a hotel, but he didn't know which one. As he was told which hotel, his mum drove him there and dropped him off. He was told which room so he calmly walked to his room. He heard some sounds coming out of his room. As he walked in, he opened his wardrobe and then... "Boo!" screamed the monster.

"Argh!" said Alex. He ran out of the room and he ended up outside. He looked behind, the monster was gone!

Evie Arkinstall (9)
Greswell Primary School & Nursery, Denton

WORLD WAR Z!

Once, there was a boy called Devon and in his country there was a zombie war and if you got bitten, you turned into one! To get out, he decided to go on a plane but on the plane, there was a zombie so he had to crash! Unfortunately, a piece of metal got stuck in his hip.

Later, Devon went to the hospital but in a secret box he'd found there was a formula that killed zombies. He told the police to use it and all the zombies were killed. They all lived happily ever after.

Phoebe Lovesconte (9)
Greswell Primary School & Nursery, Denton

THE DEATH CHASE...

Walking back home, Katie noticed something on the other side of the bare field, something that she'd never seen before. A circus. She went to investigate. "What is this place?" she wondered as she examined the mirrors closely. They were covered in dust and grime. "So hygienic!" she mumbled sarcastically. Something appeared behind her and immediately, she froze. A clown stood by her shoulder. "Hello there, Katie!" he grinned. Slowly, she turned around. He was gone. He was in the mirrors, grinning menacingly. "Thank you for your time, buh-bye!" she cried as she dashed out.
Nobody saw her again...

Chloe Walmsley-Taylor (10)
Mesne Lea Primary School, Worsley

THE RIPPER'S REVENGE

"How long until we've found the blood bags Brother?" spoke Rebecca. The hospital was dark because it was closed and the power went out. Long, dark corridors led to empty or full rooms. Elijah spoke to Rebecca, "Patience Rebecca, we must wait for Niklaus to find them himself."

Finally, they reached a cooler so Elijah opened it. "Ugh, Brother, I don't remember you leaving Father's stake in the cooler next to the blood bags," spoke Elijah, but Niklaus didn't listen.

He opened it anyway.

"Niklaus! Stop!" yelled Elijah...

Stab! "We have to run, now!" yelled Niklaus.

Kianoosh Moshini Zavieh (10)
Mesne Lea Primary School, Worsley

WELCOME TO THE FUNHOUSE

There I was, excited to go to the funhouse. I was with my sister. We soon arrived. There he was, the clown, standing with a smirk. He sang, "Welcome to the funhouse!"
He repeated himself. I walked on, not knowing that my sister wasn't behind me. Where could she have gone? She wasn't with the clown because he'd followed me. I tried to lose him, but I couldn't I crawled into the tunnel. There was my sister! Without warning, the clown barricaded us in. "We all float here," he whispered before disappearing.
Where he was now, nobody knew...

Millie Wright (10)
Mesne Lea Primary School, Worsley

SPOOKY SAGA

In the middle of nowhere, an abandoned hospital was there so two children went inside. They were in a corridor, they were shivering with fear. They saw something fall onto the floor. Then suddenly they saw a black figure and then it disappeared. They carried on walking, then ignored it. They finally got inside so they started to play truth or dare. Jeff said, "I dare you to sit on one of the beds and scream."

He did it. Suddenly, he saw a black figure. It had blood on it. One of the children turned around and then he fainted...

Ethan Joel Harris (9)
Mesne Lea Primary School, Worsley

THE BREAK-IN OF THE PRISON

CJ and Emil were walking back from school and it was a dark and gloomy night. They couldn't see a thing. They found a building and they entered it. First, they checked upstairs to find some help and directions. When they reached the top of the stairs, they heard iron chains rattling. They slowly approached where the noise was coming from. They turned and saw an unconscious person on the floor. They walked on and forgot about it. They heard the noise again and ran back. The person was gone and off they went, running into the dark night.

Charlie Steele (9)
Mesne Lea Primary School, Worsley

STUCK IN THE STAIRCASE

At eleven o'clock on a Sunday morning, Daisy was going to get some breakfast. Then she fell down the hole in the broken staircase. It was dusty and dingy inside the staircase. In one particular corner of the staircase, there was a mountain of cobwebs and, every few seconds, it moved. Daisy banged on the wall but the cobwebs kept moving. Slowly but surely, each of the cobwebs started falling to the ground. When the cobwebs all fell to the ground, it revealed a young boy who'd lived there before. They both wondered how to get out...

Amelia Pimlott (10)
Mesne Lea Primary School, Worsley

THE REVENGE OF THE POT DOLL

Jade's hair stood on end as the cold floor sent shivers down her spine. There were no windows or doors and, as she lay in the dark corridor, Jade saw her worst nightmare. The stench of death lingered in the air, but what concerned her the most was the pot doll. She tried to scream but nothing came out. Jade's heart pounded and suddenly the doll was gone. Blood dripped from the ceiling. Jade, using all her courage, looked up. She ran again but froze. Jade grabbed the doll and threw it. She was safe! She could finally go home!

Sienna-Rose Millership (10)
Mesne Lea Primary School, Worsley

STUCK IN A SHED

As Timmy entered the abandoned shed, he instantly regretted playing truth or dare. Timmy nervously pushed the ancient door open. There was a chill as he stepped into the shed. *Bang!* The door slammed behind him. He was shaking, he'd left the keys outside and there was nothing but cobwebs inside. He started to panic. He had no one to help him. Timmy looked over to the window and spotted a black figure. He ducked down next to piles of boxes and turned around. There he was with a bat, dripping with lots of blood...

Joshua Thomas Whitehead (9)
Mesne Lea Primary School, Worsley

THE SHADOW

Hope was playing hide-and-seek until she saw an abandoned house. The haunted house looked like it had been on fire. The little girl went in the abandoned house, terrified and curious. Her hands started sweating. Hope saw a plant pot with webs all around it. Webs were also in the corners of the house. Suddenly, she heard a noise! In the blink of an eye, a shadow appeared. Hope's heart started beating faster. She turned around and saw nothing. She turned around again and saw a person dressed in black, holding a knife...

Beatriz De Ataide (9)
Mesne Lea Primary School, Worsley

MURDERER!

As I entered the dark, gloomy room, I felt a frosty shiver that clambered up my spine. Dust devoured the room. Meanwhile, I was trembling. There was barely anything inside, all there was was a cracked window and a door that opened with a terrifying creak! Without warning, the door was gone! I tried to rub my eyes but I was too frightened. My heart started to beat faster and I started to breathe heavily. Terrifyingly, I saw a red liquid drop from the ceiling. I looked up and I saw a man with a knife in his bloodied head...

Joshua Anthony Clarke (10)
Mesne Lea Primary School, Worsley

THE THING!

It was Halloween night and there was a disco.
A girl was reading her spooky stories to people.
They got home and got a little thing.
A day later, the little thing was on the landing.
Mum was confused. Zoey came out crying, "I can't sleep!"
Mum put the doll in her room. That night, the thing was somehow flat on the mum's face!
She was screaming, "Argh! Argh! Argh!"
The girl ran in and the doll put a spell on Zoey and her mum. Monsters came out of nowhere. They both fainted...

Oscar Bruce Bentley (10)
Mesne Lea Primary School, Worsley

FEAR!

She waded out of the shadows and instantly, mist wrapped around her bare arms. She was in the middle of nowhere, planting her bony legs into the numbingly cold water. She glanced back from where she had come, but it was too late. Darkness had already swallowed her tracks. She could feel the fear like a coiled spring in the pit of her stomach. She knew the ghosts were coming for her. Then, she saw something in the corner of her eye. It was a figure. It came closer and grabbed her. Terrified, she hit back and ran away!

Alexa Noon (10)
Mesne Lea Primary School, Worsley

VAMPIRE WORMS

In the forest where scary creatures and beasts were, a person went inside. It was very dark. He tripped over a rock and he saw vampire worms on the grass that ate people. He saw a lot of vampire worms so he ran back to his house, but there were more vampire worms. The person had no idea how those creatures got there, but he went to escape quickly. The vampire worms were catching up with him, he wasn't fast enough! The person decided to trap the worms with his basket so they wouldn't get out.

Luis Alfredo Paredes (10)

Mesne Lea Primary School, Worsley

THE LAST GIRL

Camilla was in her room, she was listening to music on her phone with blue headphones. There was arguing coming from downstairs because Camilla's dad broke her mum's favourite cup. It went on for at least thirty minutes. Mum said, "I want a new one!"
"Fine, I'll get you one."
While she was listening to her music, there was a big bang and a clown popped up on her phone. Then there was a tap on her shoulder, but there was nothing there. She fainted.

Ellie Brooks (10)
Mesne Lea Primary School, Worsley

BLACK JACKET BOY!

I was going trick or treating with my friends. I went round to my friend's house and knocked on his door, saying, "Come on!"
We left and went around half of the houses. Nobody had ever knocked on the last house on my street since the massive house fire when two children had passed away. Me and my friends all knocked on the door and there was no answer so we looked through the smashed window and it was pitch-black. I looked through the peephole and somebody was there...

Lennox Dacha (10)
Mesne Lea Primary School, Worsley

THE OTHER SIDE OF PONGY PEPPA

Peppa Pig found an abandoned cave with dangerous vampire bats. Out of nowhere, Noah the ninja came and fly-kicked Peppa Pig in the face. She checked her bag for nunchucks but it had a doll in it. The doll jumped out of the bag and tried to hit Pongy Peppa. Like a monkey, Tarzan flew in and whacked the doll. From the sky came Mary Poppins with her umbrella. She was like a goddess. Daddy Pig came flying through the sky and did a massive snort; it made half of the world break apart and die!

Dylan Mallalieu (10)
Mesne Lea Primary School, Worsley

THE MONSTER

One dark, starry night, I was exploring an abandoned house. There was an attic, so I explored it. There was a tall figure near the attic door, clocking it so I couldn't get out. I looked away and looked back, he was gone! I was petrified! I looked everywhere and still nothing. I shouted, "Hello!" hoping for an answer.

I froze like a statue. I saw the monster getting closer and closer until he grabbed me. He got a claw to my neck. I screamed. I was never seen again.

Ted Crank (9)
Mesne Lea Primary School, Worsley

THE PRISON BREAK

Adam was walking onto his street. He saw a den and it said: *Free Sweets Here,* so he went inside. He stepped in and the door shut and locked behind him. Adam went inside a spiralling tunnel and he realised that it was a jail. There was blood on the walls and nail marks. He looked inside one of the cells and saw that there was a man. He carried on but he didn't know that the man had broken out and had started to follow him around the prison. He looked behind him and ran...

Rahimah Seriki (9)
Mesne Lea Primary School, Worsley

TERRIFYING GRAVEYARD!

There was a boy called Elliott having a stroll in the graveyard. Everything was dull. A shadow caught Elliott's eye. He turned around, there was a vampire with new, red blood dripping from his mouth. He had black hair and fangs like a gargantuan shark. The graves in the graveyard had blood splattered all over them. Elliott's heart was pounding as he was staring into the devil's eyes. Elliott tried to escape but he stumbled backwards while the vampire zoomed past him...

Austin Humphreys (9)
Mesne Lea Primary School, Worsley

PRISON BREAK

Me and Grace woke up, we were trapped in a cell. Grace found a key. I said, "Try looking for a safe or a door."
Me and Grace opened the door, we looked around for some clues. Then, *bang!* In the cafe, we saw a smashed plate. Just then I saw a mask behind the counter. Me and Grace went to the counter. I said, "Ugh, cobwebs..."
Then I saw the Game Master. He chased us and when the Game Master caught us, we were never seen again...

Alfie James Cox (9)
Mesne Lea Primary School, Worsley

ABANDONED HOUSE

Ruby and Mia walked past a haunted house. Mia dared Ruby to go in so she opened the door for her to go inside. Mia asked if they could go upstairs but she ran up without Ruby. Ruby checked the kitchen and found knives on the table with blood covering them. Ruby ran upstairs and saw a closed door. She opened it and Mia was tied up in a chair! A guy wore a mask, covered in blood, and had a chainsaw. He turned around and saw Ruby. Ruby screamed, "Argh!"

Maria Juliette Staniecka (9)
Mesne Lea Primary School, Worsley

THE CLOWN

Me and Mark woke up in a freaky, weird, abandoned hospital and, what made me worry even more was that there were no patients. It seemed that we were the only ones there. Mark called for nurses but nobody replied so I got out of bed. I saw the creepiest thing in my life: a clown with a massive knife. The worst bit was that he had a knocked-out nurse over his shoulder. He tried to kill me but I dodged him and then Mark grabbed the clown and stabbed it.

Kayden Thompson (11)
Mesne Lea Primary School, Worsley

COME OUT

In a mansion, a boy called Max was playing on his PS4. He was soon bored so he went downstairs to get something to eat. He went back and saw a person holding his controller but Max had no idea who it was. Max's face was cold with tears. He was home alone and felt like his skin was falling off. When Max saw him, he ran around the shiny, gold floor. Max ran into a cupboard and hid. The person said, "Come out, come out wherever you are!"

Oligen Mutanya (9)
Mesne Lea Primary School, Worsley

THE CASTLE'S ATTIC

At a forbidden, scary castle, there was a girl called Anna and her friends who played hide-and-seek. Anna went to hide with two of her friends. When they went to hide, they were saying to themselves, "They will never find us here!"
They were hiding in the attic. While they were there, they got scared. They tried to open the door but it was locked. The lights started to flicker on and off, then they saw a black figure...

Kyron Earith (9)
Mesne Lea Primary School, Worsley

THE GAME MASTER

Me and Kayden woke up in an abandoned cell with rusty, old bars and gloomy floorboards. The walls were spray-painted and covered with spiderwebs. Then we broke out and played hide-and-seek. Kayden was counting. I went running and saw a mask zoom past me. I shouted to Kayden, but he didn't answer me. I just carried on walking to my hiding spot. I saw it again, it was the Game Master. I was never seen again...

Mark Redshaw (10)
Mesne Lea Primary School, Worsley

THE MYSTERIOUS CAVE

As the sky was dark, my dad and I were exploring a cave. We entered the cave. "Argh! Bats!" I shouted.

There were loads of bats in the cave. I heard a noise. "Dad? What was that?"

"Argh! Run!"

"Dad! There's a vampire!"

My dad and I ran as fast as we could.

"Ha, you think you can trick me?"

"No, we can't!" said my dad.

"Yes we can," I said.

"How dare you, little girl!" The vampire was about to bite us and... "Pranked you!"

It was my mum.

"Mum! You scared me!"

I'd forgotten about Halloween.

Astou Mbow (10)
Oasis Academy Harpur Mount, Harpurhey

BASEMENT

Flashbacks flashed through Meg's head. "Don't go down there!" yelled the matron.
"Why?" replied the children.
"I said don't go in there!"
In the middle of the night, Meg and a boy called Tim sneaked down to a small elevator.
"Ready?" said Meg.
"Ready," said Tim. Meg pressed the button. Tim went down.
"Why am I going down?" yelled Tim. Meg was pushing the button repeatedly. Tim was on the bottom floor, something was there... "Argh!" It had one arm and a body and a head.
Meg woke up and in front of her was the monster that killed Tim...

Joel Preston (10)
Oasis Academy Harpur Mount, Harpurhey

THE ABANDONED HOUSE

It was a long, hard day; me, lily and Astou were going down the old country lane and saw an abandoned cottage. We went down the stairs into the basement and looked for things. We found a note on the old, rickety table. It said: 'Tell all your friends goodbye tonight because you might die if you don't follow these rules correctly!'
Lilly said, "There's someone over there..."
Astou said, "Why did you say that? Now you've given me the shivers!"
Then the person jumped out, "Ha, ha, ha! Happy Halloween!"
The man said, "Is it really?" under his breath...

Kasey Christine Jackson (10)
Oasis Academy Harpur Mount, Harpurhey

THE STORY OF THE TEENAGE GIRL DAISY!

As the sun shone down on Daisy's house, her dad told her to check the church. She went to get her new rainbow bike and went down the rough path. She explored around her when she went down a hill. When she finally got there, the church door was open. She walked towards the door and walked in slowly. She explored and heard a voice. "Daisy?"
"Yeah?" she said. She walked towards the voice. It was a ghost! Approaching it, she pulled the sheet off. "Dad?" she questioned.
"Yeah?" he said.
"Why are you here?"
"I'm waiting for you," he replied.

Jessica Anglin (11)
Oasis Academy Harpur Mount, Harpurhey

THE STORY OF LOCKDOWN

Walking into the classroom, "Oh no! I'm late again!"
We were already in the middle of maths, I sat down in my seat and started writing. The whole class was learning algebra. While I was writing, Mrs Gibson got a message on the walkie-talkie.
"Lockdown!"
Mr Magoweon and Miss Celebon stacked tables and chairs against the door, Mrs Gibson helped us hide and be quiet. All we could hear was gunshots. They came to our classroom. Everyone was silent. They came to our door, one of them shot the door. "Argh!" Jessica screamed.
They came in... "Help us! Argh!"

Tessie McGowan (10)
Oasis Academy Harpur Mount, Harpurhey

THE RETURN

Guess what? The Swampy-Swiper was back! He was attacking the town with his army and his lieutenant (his son). They sneaked into the barracks and captured some guards and interrogated them. "Where is the mit?" asked Swampy.

"It's in the palace!"

After they were told the information, they headed to the palace to find the mit, but Ethan the paladin jumped them and started to attack. "Why are you attacking us? All we want is peace!"

Swampy knew what a mistake he'd made. He then made a promise to help all and protect the mit and the land...

Dayton Toby (11)
Oasis Academy Harpur Mount, Harpurhey

UNDER THE MECHANICAL SEA

Waking up, I found myself on an old, rusty ship. I sprinted upstairs and peered over the metal rails. I spotted a grey, vicious shark swimming towards me through the murky, blue ocean. *Chomp! Chomp! Chomp!* It was ripping the boat apart with ease. Within seconds, the beast was inches away from my feet. Suddenly, I spotted wires in the monster's mouth. I touched the shark and realised it was an animatronic programmed to frighten unaware humans! I looked over the rails, still unable to believe what happened. Suddenly, I saw a grey, small fin slowly coming towards me...

Raya Renay Higgins (11)
Oasis Academy Harpur Mount, Harpurhey

A WALK THROUGH THE PARK

Jeff pelted through the park, hearing noises.
"What was that?" he asked.
Sounds echoed from every direction. Exploring every bit of the park, ravens screaming, billions of them above. Suddenly, a chainsaw came out of a bush and lay, motionless. "Argh!"
The serial killer tried to grab Jeff but missed. Leaping away, he grabbed his chainsaw and began chasing him. Jeff falling to the ground, he caught up, raised his chainsaw and pointed it at Jeff. Jeff recognised him and pulled his mask off... It was the kidnapper who'd taken his sister!

Krystian Mikolaj Maciejewski (11)
Oasis Academy Harpur Mount, Harpurhey

CELEBRITY SCARE

Bang! In a flash of light, a huge meteor crashed in the middle of a suspicious forest. The news reporters went to record the huge meteor - everyone wanted to see it. But when they watched the footage back, they caught a dark, suspicious figure. They told the police and the police went hunting for the dark figure...
Bang! The figure made a loud noise. "Argh!" a girl started to scream.
The police found the dark figure and it turned out that the figure was a costume and David Beckham was the one wearing it! Everyone laughed loudly.

Ricardo Singh (10)
Oasis Academy Harpur Mount, Harpurhey

NEVER EVER TRUST YOUR FRIENDS

A fourteen-year-old boy called Peter walked through a spooky forest. Exploring, he saw a haunted house. He investigated the antique artefacts, dolls and rickety chairs. It got darker and darker. Suddenly, the lights went out and it was pitch-black. Trying to gather materials to make light was a tough challenge for him. He needed help desperately. He thought to himself. From out of nowhere, creepy zombies appeared, moving closer and closer to the house. As fast as the Flash, he ran down the stairs and found out it was his friends, remembering that it was Halloween.

Doyin Adedeji (10)
Oasis Academy Harpur Mount, Harpurhey

A BOY AND A FRIENDLY GHOST

On a lonely night, a boy was sleeping in a blue bed and he heard clicking on his brown wardrobe. He jumped out of bed and opened it. A white, floating ghost jumped out and whispered, "I'm a friendly ghost!"

All day long, they played in the bedroom with action figures and on the boy's PS4. At the end of the day, the boy's dad jumped out of the white, floating ghost costume. "Happy Halloween!" exclaimed the dad.

The boy couldn't believe his dad had pranked him. He waited until he could get his dad back next Halloween...

Jake Cutler (11)
Oasis Academy Harpur Mount, Harpurhey

THE HAUNTING HALLWAY

This was my first day in my new primary school. The first lesson was science (I hated science and maths). During science, I met an extraordinary girl called Rose. Sadly, the next day, Rose wasn't in and I had no one to play with or talk to. Walking down the corridor, I realised that nobody was there. Suddenly, the lockers started slamming. I made a run for it. A few hours later, the same thing happened but this time, Rose jumped out of my dark blue locker. "Happy birthday!" she shouted. This was the best birthday I'd ever experienced.

Ruby Davies (10)
Oasis Academy Harpur Mount, Harpurhey

MOVING ANGEL

A boy called Arthur Thompson was strolling down an abandoned street. He stumbled across a bright blue telephone booth and walked towards it. Walking in, it was pitch-black. The lights turned on; there were stone statues and a row of doors. Exploring, he noticed the winged statue was gone. Swiftly, he turned... it was there! He rubbed his eyes. It was gone!
Arthur screamed, sprinting to the nearest door. He was terrified. The lights flickered, it was there, holding an object. What was it...? He looked closer. It was some delicious, mouth-watering candy!

Lewis Arthur Thompson (10)
Oasis Academy Harpur Mount, Harpurhey

TRICK OR TREAT?

Halloween - the best day ever had arrived. After a boring day at school, I went home. Two hours later, I went to the school's Halloween party. When I arrived, there were lots of students from school. Suddenly, I saw two scary people staring at me strangely. They whispered to each other and walked towards me. I was scared, they were vampires and zombies! I ran quickly and they ran after me with a bucket. Did they have poisonous candy? I found a sweet stand and hid behind it. They looked. I accidentally sneezed. They said, "Trick or treat?"

Umer Nadeem (11)
Oasis Academy Harpur Mount, Harpurhey

THE SHACK

Walking through the murky forest, towering trees over my head, my bike crunched on the branches. There was my friend, he exclaimed, "We shouldn't go to the forest. Some people died here, they got possessed!"
There was a little shack in the middle of the forest. I opened the door, it slammed behind me. I was locked in! I heard a chainsaw. Someone threw rocks and the glass shattered. The chainsaw cracked the door. There were men in black suits and women in black suits. When they took off their masks, I was confused... "Mum!"

Daniyal Khan (10)
Oasis Academy Harpur Mount, Harpurhey

SCHOOL

One day, Bell and Apple-White were going to school. Suddenly, a zombie scared them. They ran to the pool, the zombie chased them but he was sick, so they pushed him into the pool and when the zombie entered the pool, he was destroyed. There were lots more zombies to destroy, but Bell and Apple-White were cunning, they got the other zombies and pushed them into the pool.

When they all melted in the water, the principal was happy. The principal said, "No school for both Bell and Apple-White because they are the heroes of the school."

Isabel Hope Nichols (11)

Oasis Academy Harpur Mount, Harpurhey

HOMEWORK AND HALLOWEEN

Today was the day of the Halloween party at my all-girls school. I came to school dressed in my all-black uniform. Strange things were moving around the 500-year-old school, it was Halloween so it was normal. During lesson time, there was a black and white shadow zooming around the walls. As I went to the bathroom, there was a jack-o'-lantern and it kept moving.

Finally, it was the end of school so I got ready. Something didn't feel right. I turned around to see a teacher carrying a mountain of homework! "Argh!"

Fateenah Eniola Soneye (11)
Oasis Academy Harpur Mount, Harpurhey

THE LONELY MONSTER

There was once a monster called Joel. He always wanted to have friends but he didn't have any because he was big and scary. The smelly monster only had a dog called Bob. One day, Joel went to a nearby, beautiful village to find some friends. After a while, he found some kind, caring friends. His new mates helped him smell amazing by giving him a spray called Deodorant. He and his dog, Bob, went out to a concert and he made more friends because Joel smelled appealing. Joel and Bob now had friends and smelled good.

Skye Tyson (11)
Oasis Academy Harpur Mount, Harpurhey

THE DAY OF THE DEAD...

Coming back from school, me and Bob were playing. We were walking down a road and I noticed an abandoned house. Bob screamed, "Don't go!"
"Why?"
He said his uncle had died there, so I went inside alone. I opened the door, spiderwebs were everywhere. Cautiously, I stepped in, I fell into a hole and saw a figure in front of me, holding candy. I was confused. I remembered it was Halloween today. The figure moved his mask and it was my friend, Dave. It was all just a prank that Bob made.

Musa Waqas (10)
Oasis Academy Harpur Mount, Harpurhey

THE GIANT AND THE CANDY

Together, with my pet dragon, I went to explore an abandoned city on the other side of the island. As we arrived, I noticed a huge shadow on the ground. A giant stood in front of me, his body was green and an eyepatch covered his eye. His intentions were clear, he wanted to kill us! As fast as lightning, we started running. In a shop, we found the perfect weapon: infecting candy. I set up a trap.
When the giant approached us, he picked up the candy. He sniffed it and he ate it. He collapsed on the ground.

Ricardas Balciunas (11)
Oasis Academy Harpur Mount, Harpurhey

CINEMA DISASTER

Tim headed to the cinema with his friends, happy to watch the new film. They sat down but the cinema was abandoned, lights out... Frightened and sat in the dark, Tim and his friends had no clue what to do. The screen came on, but there was no one there. A monster was on the screen. It was a shadow. They ran around the cinema and at the popcorn stand was a fluffy werewolf eating the popcorn. It turned around and came after them. Running at the monster, they pushed him into the popcorn box and shut it!

Thomas Jackson (11)
Oasis Academy Harpur Mount, Harpurhey

FOREST ADVENTURES

I was fast asleep, dreaming of being an explorer. I woke up. Opening my mum and dad's room, I found them sleeping. Like a snail, I went downstairs, ate my cereal, got my coat and looked for the house keys. I knew they would be in Dad's room...

Going up, entering the room, the door creaked, but I didn't mind. I went to the forest, I wanted to know what creatures were there. I began to go deeper into the forest, but I wanted to go back. Suddenly, my house appeared in the forest!

Abdullah Omar Shawish (10)
Oasis Academy Harpur Mount, Harpurhey

FRANCIS

Francis was at an old, abandoned lake. She walked slowly into the woods. She heard a snap behind her, there was a killer! She heard a creak. She turned around, the killer chased her. Suddenly, she fell into the water and the killer jumped in. She swam around and he slowly chased after her. She jumped out of the water, then the killer followed her, running after her. The killer caught up to her. She saw that it was her boyfriend and then remembered that it was Halloween!

Mason Lewis (10)
Oasis Academy Harpur Mount, Harpurhey

DIE OR DIE PAINFULLY

"This place is creepy," shivered Aderyn.

"My grandpa died sixteen days after he visited Kids' Haunted House."

"'Kids Haunted House' has sixteen letters..." whispered Julia.

"Really?" whimpered Aderyn.

"Maybe it's a coincidence?" said Julia. They entered the haunted house.

"Welcome to the haunted house! You will never come out!" boomed an invisible voice.

"Oh my! That axe looks so real!" screamed Aderyn.

"That's because it is real!" whispered Julia as it sliced a person in half. They were next.

"Prepare to die!" said a wild, invisible voice. Maniacal laughter filled the dark, cursed room...

Irene Momoh (10)
St Anthony's Catholic Primary School, Wythenshawe

SLENDER MAN AND THE 8 PAGES

There were three friends: Orange, Pear and Grapefruit. Grapefruit heard a voice, "Go to the forest and collect eight pages."
"I'll go to the forest and get the pages," he said.
Grapefruit went missing. "Where's Grapefruit?" said Orange.
"In the forest," Pear answered. "Slender Man lives there. He kills anyone who doesn't find the eight pages in a minute."
They went to the forest. Orange found four pages, Pear found the others. "We did it!"
Slender Man came and said, "Congratulations, you found the pages. I'll give you your friend back." He disappeared and the three friends went home happily.

Stephan Kurian (8)
St Anthony's Catholic Primary School, Wythenshawe

THAT THING IN THE SHED

There once were two girls called Maddie and Angel. They were inseparable twins. They loved each other very much. One night, they heard a noise. It was coming from the shed. It was a scary noise. They went to investigate and opened the shed door. There was nothing there. "It could have been the invisible boy," said Angel.

"The invisible boy isn't real," said Maddie.

They took a step forward, the door shut and locked from the outside. "Argh!" shrieked both girls.

"There's a light switch here," said Angel. She flicked the switch.

"What's that?"

"Rar!" the thing roared...

Scarlett Cork (9)

St Anthony's Catholic Primary School, Wythenshawe

THE DEADLY BLERWRENCH

A long time ago, in a cold and creepy cottage lived the deadliest Blerwrench. Blerwrenches were creatures, half-wolf, half-horse. As the moonlight shone upon the cottage, a dark figure appeared. It was a Blerwrench!
The door slowly opened and made a loud creak as I entered the room. "Hello?" came a voice from behind me.
"Who's there? Who is it? Show yourself!"
The Blerwrench slowly appeared. As the Blerwrench came to my attention, he roared as loud as he could.
"Don't hurt me please!" I said, shivering in the corner of the room.
"Got you!"

Katie Elorm Mensah (9)
St Anthony's Catholic Primary School, Wythenshawe

THE STORY OF THE KILLER, LILLY!

Deep in the dark woods, there was a venomous, bloodsucking vampire called Killer Lilly. This mysterious creature would hide under the dark bed in children's rooms and give them nightmares.

One dark day, while Killer Lilly was looking for a house, her eyes lit up as she saw a vicious vampire boy. She walked up to him and said, "Hello."

He said, "Hi, my name's Killer Zack."

Killer Lilly said, "Do you want to be friends?"

"Yes," said Zack. Killer Lilly and Killer Zack were best friends forever and ever, they never left each other.

Kioni Hannaway (7)
St Anthony's Catholic Primary School, Wythenshawe

GRAVEYARD MADNESS

One really spooky night, a girl called Miley was trick or treating, then she walked into an eerie graveyard to get to the next neighbourhood. Miley kept on walking until she came across her auntie's grave. When she came across her auntie's grave, she started getting haunted! Her auntie didn't like her, so her ghosts started haunting Miley!

After Halloween, Miley kept getting her homework, poems and bed destroyed by her auntie's ghost. Her auntie kept haunting her until Miley found a potion to take ghosts away. Miley drank the potion and that was the end of the hauntings!

Sandra Wlodarczyk (9)
St Anthony's Catholic Primary School, Wythenshawe

THE MYSTERIOUS SHADOW

I opened the door of the abandoned haunted house which was in the middle of nowhere. I looked around the corner to see a dark, tall shadow on the crusty, half-painted wall. I looked around and saw nobody. Where was the shadow coming from? Who else was in this house?
Suddenly, I heard a whisper saying, "Hello Laura."
I said, "Who is that?"
The loud, deep voice said, "Look behind you."
I rapidly turned around. Nothing was there. The door loudly slammed shut. I quickly opened the door, ran out of the house but, something began to follow me...

Panashe Musungwa (10)
St Anthony's Catholic Primary School, Wythenshawe

THE MISSING FOOTBALLER

Liam Malfoy just scored City's second goal. They were two-one up. All the fans were screaming and cheering, they were all very excited. Liam had that sinister feeling, he was puzzled. Unfortunately, twenty minutes later, they were drawing. Luckily, in stoppage time, Malfoy scored. The fans were going crazy. City won, four-three. In the changing room, the players were going delirious. Everybody was out of the changing room, except Liam. The door was locked. Had Liam gone out? He was missing! They were searching for days. Funnily, he'd gone searching for his lost boots! Silly Liam!

Olivia Mulvey (10)
St Anthony's Catholic Primary School, Wythenshawe

MYSTERY

One creepy night, Frankenstein dragged his feet along the path and crept into the haunted house where me and all my creepy friends had been waiting for a haunting week.

The next dreadful morning, we all had eyeball and worm soup. After breakfast, we went to discover a haunted, dreadful house just to see if we could live there. When we went in, we heard footsteps coming from a horrible bedroom. We all ran out of the spooky, terrifying house, all the way to the horrible house underground. Frankenstein met an ugly ghost that couldn't see and they became friends.

Alfie Hackney (7)
St Anthony's Catholic Primary School, Wythenshawe

MEMORIES FROM THE DARK

Spookily, the transparent spirit rose from its coffin labelled 'Jeremy Agar'. He recognised where he was: he was in the graveyard, next to his mother's grave who'd died when he was ten years old. An old man walked past with flowers. He didn't see the spirit, then the spirit recognised that it was dead. He remembered who killed him. The spirit wanted revenge. The spirit was now evil, he went to everyone who'd hurt him during his life. He tormented each one, one by one, and then returned to his dusty coffin to rest until next time...

Takudaishe Musungua (7)
St Anthony's Catholic Primary School, Wythenshawe

THE HORRIFYING HEADLESS HORSEMAN

There once was a corn maze. It was Halloween night, there was a girl who was lost. Frightened, the scared girl heard loud hooves trotting, but it was only her in the maze. It was 3am, it was as dark as a 2,000ft hole. The girl screamed at the top of her lungs. The horrifying lightning went *crash! Boom!* The scared girl remembered she'd read a book about the headless horseman, who haunted this maze on Halloween night at 3am. Someone grabbed the girl, it was the headless horseman! Not a single soul ever saw her again.

Rosie McMahon (8)
St Anthony's Catholic Primary School, Wythenshawe

FORGOT PHANTOM

The dark forest's trees are surrounding me. I have no hope to escape. I've been screaming for help until I see this strange creature. It's tall, a man maybe? He's as pale as snow and wearing a dark suit and a red tie and has eight tentacles. He's coming!

Now, where is he? He's teleported! I'd better run now! There's no mercy from this phantom. I try to miss the branches, but it's no use, my face is stinging. He's here! There's no hope for me. I'm dead with the phantom.

Mateusz Steczkiewicz (10)
St Anthony's Catholic Primary School, Wythenshawe

IN A HAUNTED HOUSE

I had finally woken up. When I woke up, blood was pouring from where I lay. Did anybody know where I was? Imagine a place where blood was pouring, where nightmares came true, where everybody came to life: this spooky haunted house. I said "Hello" in a quiet voice and as I said hello, a vampire and a ghost approached me in an odd kind of way.
I didn't know what to do, should I run or should I scream? I was puzzled. I slowly turned around and as I did the vampire scared me. It was only my brother!

Amira Lydia Brew-Butler (9)
St Anthony's Catholic Primary School, Wythenshawe

THE SCARY THING

Once upon a time, there was a boy called Arthur and he was a scared boy. He had lots of dreams about monsters. In the morning, he was screaming because there was a zombie in front of him. The zombie grabbed him and said, "Let me eat you!"

The boy ran into another zombie that said, "Let me eat you."

Arthur ran deeper into the woods and found a tree. He climbed it. The zombies tried to get him, but he was too high up. The boy called Arthur eventually came down and was eaten.

Lord Michael Ojage (8)
St Anthony's Catholic Primary School, Wythenshawe

THE OGRE AND THE BEARDED MOUNTAIN

Once upon a time, there lived some children and a grandad. The grandad told them a story. As he began the story, his beard started to grow. Niki noticed it. It felt like silk. The beard grew and Niki got lost in it. Then, he saw a cave. Inside was an ogre and he was keeping children prisoner for food! Niki saved the children from the ogre. Around the ogre's neck was a pair of scissors. He broke them and the ogre turned into a man. They all returned to the village and they lived happily ever after!

Mahimsa Gallenahene Mohottala (8)
St Anthony's Catholic Primary School, Wythenshawe

SLENDER MAN THE TERRORISER

Once upon a time, there was a boy called
Miguel. He was eleven years old and lived in a
hotel. One day, when he was asleep, he heard
a breathing noise. He got out of bed, no one
was there so he went to sleep. He was really
scared so he had a torch. Miguel heard the
same noise, but this time there was a long
shadow. He was shaking so he wanted to scare
it. He decided not to so, when Miguel walked
back, a big man with a white mask took him
away. Nobody knew what had happened...

Rodrigo Mendes (9)
St Anthony's Catholic Primary School, Wythenshawe

THE DARK, SPOOKY NIGHT TO MORNING

One spooky, dark night the vampire and his friend, the ghost saw a spooky house over the road. They went over the road and walked into the front garden and when they got closer to the spooky door a big, scary face looked out with one eye. The empty eye socket had a worm that popped out with blood dripping out. It snatched them out of the garden. They were in there until morning because something happened and they were thrown out the door with a lot of dust and fluff on them.

Alicia Louise Jasmine Tyler (7)
St Anthony's Catholic Primary School, Wythenshawe

HAUNTED GHOSTLY HOUSE

When I arrived at the old, abandoned house, I felt so scared. I felt like I just wanted to run back to my mum's house. It looked like nobody had used this house for ages. It had ripped walls, old, cracked, rusty floors... I decided to go in.

When I knocked on the door, it opened on its own. Just then, I went in. A vampire was in front of me and it said, "My lunch!"

I was scared until Wonder Girl came and killed the vampire. I was so happy!

Sofia Evangeline Daniel (9)
St Anthony's Catholic Primary School, Wythenshawe

THE HORRIBLE, SCARY, UGLY MONSTER!

It was a dark night, Jack and Sam were sleeping when suddenly, a big bang came. The attic door opened and closed. Jack and Sam both woke up in shock and they heard screaming and spooky voices. They quickly ran up to explore and see what was going on in the attic.

As soon as they entered, they saw a green, one-eyed, two-mouthed ghost who was eating their pet cat! When Jack and Sam saw the greedy ghost, they screamed and shouted and ran outside for help!

Ahad Khan (10)
St Anthony's Catholic Primary School, Wythenshawe

THE FLOATING PUMPKIN

One shallow, breathtaking Hallows' Eve night, two innocent friends turned up to a cursed, diseased house. "I don't think that this is a good idea..." I sighed under my cold breath. "Oh, don't be such a hedgehog!" Becky moaned. "Just because it's Halloween, doesn't mean that you can make stupid excuses."
The door creaked open. I shook with fear while my palms sweated. "So, who's going in?" asked Becky.
"Not me!" I screeched.
We both walked in. A floating pumpkin shouted, "Who's been intruding on my territory?"
We ran and promised not to disturb the house again!

Eunice Kipila Moungala (10)
St Barnabas CE Primary Academy, Manchester

WELCOME TO THE PARTY

I tightly gripped the note in my sweaty palms. This house had loomed menacingly over the city for years, legend had it, whoever came here never returned. Slowly, I tiptoed up the stairs as they crumbled beneath me. An evil-devouring creature crawled up my spine as I stepped onto the welcome mat, but it wasn't very welcoming. The trees' fingers pulled me into their cold, unpleasant embrace. Whispers travelled around the suffocating air. Bold, threatening gargoyles glared at me. An eerie light flickered on and I was pulled in. "Welcome to the party," my cousin sang joyfully.

Olivia Louise Donaldson (11)
St Barnabas CE Primary Academy, Manchester

THE HAUNTED MIGHTY HOUSE

Trembling with rage, I stood in front of a gruesome, sinister mansion with its roof stretching out like a neck. I inspected my surroundings and I felt a tingle that ran down my spine. The trees grinned with their rotten leaves as they swayed, whispering softly. I tottered up the mossy, gritty, many stairs as they creaked slowly. I hastily knocked on the door with sweaty palms, tiptoeing inside and seeing clear, steady mirrors. Petrified, I made my way onto the haunted, shallow floor of the house. I looked at my reflection in the mirror, but it changed...

Emmanuella Esther Anazodo (11)
St Barnabas CE Primary Academy, Manchester

HELP ME!

One night, a mysterious robber approached and ran straight through the door. He wanted to get out before 12:00. It was 11:59. The enormous clock struck 12:00. A creepy man appeared behind him. He was wearing a torn-open suit and he had a bag over his head with chains all over the bag. The robber ran out of the house and again, the creepy man appeared. He touched him and the robber turned into whatever grim nightmare he was. After a few days, nobody came to search for the robber. He realised there was no way out. "Help me!"

Cordell Stratton (10)
St Barnabas CE Primary Academy, Manchester

THE SINISTER CEMETERY

Nobody ever went to the cemetery, ever! I had to, I had to take a shortcut after a long day of work. No one went there in the dark, never! I walked through the gloomy, sinister cemetery. I heard a rustling noise. I turned, it sounded like the leaves were whispering and telling me to come closer and closer. I walked even further into the cemetery. Suddenly, there was a strange, rustling noise. It was a zombie! "Argh!" I screamed. I ran as fast as I could. They were everywhere I looked, everywhere I turned and everywhere I ran!

Skye Sharkey (10)
St Barnabas CE Primary Academy, Manchester

THE MYSTERIOUS FIGURE!

One dark, traumatising night, I was asked to go to the shop. "Can't we just wait until morning?" "No!" Then, I slowly creeped out of the crooked Tudor door, making sure not a soul was around. Suddenly, a dark figure, who made my heart sink, came out of the woods. In the blink of an eye, I darted to the shop. My body started to shake, my head started to pound. The shop was shut. He got closer and closer. I started to walk home. He went to get something so I ran home. *Knock, knock, knock...*

Brandon Corcoran (11)

St Barnabas CE Primary Academy, Manchester

THE DIMENSION...

I went out one night. It was about 21:15. My mum was going to kill me, it was very late. *I will do one more house,* I thought to myself. I walked up to this house and knocked. No answer. I knocked constantly and still no answer. Strangely, the door was unlocked. I decided to go in and look all around the house. No one was to be seen. I didn't look in the bedroom, there was a strange mirror there. I kept looking at it. "Get out," someone whispered. I jumped away from the mirror and never came back.

Jorja Burns (10)
St Barnabas CE Primary Academy, Manchester

THE MYSTERIOUS HOUSE...

One night, it was Halloween. I went trick or treating. After a while, I came to a huge, abandoned mansion. I tentatively knocked. I could hear stomping footsteps creeping around. In the blink of an eye, a green, slimy hand shot out like a bullet from a gun. I was pushed into a dark, gloomy chamber. I could hear people whispering in the air. There was screaming as if there were other people in the abandoned place. I slowly crept through the house and tried to open all the doors. They just opened to the unknown...

Aiden Gettings (10)
St Barnabas CE Primary Academy, Manchester

THE CEMETERY

A long time ago, in a small town, there was a boy on Halloween night. The huge sack he was carrying would soon be full. Although it was very full, he was still able to pull it. Then, the boy saw a house in the cemetery and, daring himself, he walked in without a care. As he walked closer to the house, pumpkins blinked at him. Everybody was scared of the cemetery. The boy rang the doorbell and the window glowed. The door creaked open slightly and he was pulled in by a large hand. "Happy Halloween..."

David James (10)
St Barnabas CE Primary Academy, Manchester

LIGHTS OUT...

It was Friday 13th July at 3.30am. I felt different, very different. Something was looming, I knew it... I looked at the clock, it was 3.31am. I heard the clock go *tick-tock, tick-tock*. My heart was pounding. It felt eerie. I decided to go to bed. It was 3.32am, I turned the lights off and saw a figure. I rushed to my bed and turned on the lights. I turned the lights off again, it was 3.33am. I saw the figure, it was small... A doll. Its voice said, "We're gonna have fun..."

Amna Ahmed (11)
St Barnabas CE Primary Academy, Manchester

GRANABELLE!

One day, I was moving into a new house. As I stepped into the house, there was a temperature drop. A few minutes later, it was late at night. I went to bed. Suddenly, I heard my car starting in the garage, so I went downstairs and saw a note on my car. It said, 'Do you want to play hide-and-seek?'
I then heard my grandma's laugh. As I looked around, I saw a figure hovering over me. She had a note on her and it said: 'Help me'. All of a sudden, she disappeared...

Destiny Tamia Knight (10)
St Barnabas CE Primary Academy, Manchester

THE UNUSUAL TIME CHANGE

Helia ran away from the policeman until he bumped into another one. "Slow down buddy."
"I'm sorry, I didn't mean to kill her!"
"What are you saying? We haven't had a murder in twenty years."
"Wait, what year is this?"
"1989, why?"
"No reason," he lied and sprang off. He could see lots of years going through his head and, then it stopped. "Excuse me, what year is this?"
"2018."
His jaw dropped until he ran off again but, before he could say anything, he was sucked into another time loop and was, unfortunately, never seen again.

Elliott Andrew Backhouse (10)
St John's CE Primary School, Failsworth

THE HOUSE

Ella and her friend wandered off to the next house. They didn't realise that the next house was the abandoned house of Alexa Street, they were too busy looking at how many sweets they had. As they approached the daunting building, they heard a loud, murderous scream. They both stopped in fear, but then, Tom ran up to the door. Millie said, "No, Tom! Don't!" Ella started to pull him away, but a strange figure appeared. It was like they were pulling Tom into the house. When they went in, it was silent except for the blood-curdling screams echoing around...

Lilly Crumlish (10)
St John's CE Primary School, Failsworth

DAD!

"Trick or treat?" said the boy.
"I like your costume," said the man.
"Thanks Dad, look what I got! Erm... Dad? Where are you?"
The boy was very nervous and worried.
"Excuse me? Have you seen my dad?"
"No," replied the man.
"Oh no! What am I going to do?"
Suddenly... "Boo!"
"Argh! Dad! Why did you do that?"
"Oh, sorry, I didn't mean to scare you like that."
"It's fine, but don't do it again."
"Okay."

Oliver Duff (9)
St John's CE Primary School, Failsworth

THE ABANDONED MANSION OF HORRORS

Four girls, Sophie, Ferne, L'Nayah and Ariarna sneaked into the Mansion of Horrors. They walked up to the door and it swung open. No one was there. The girls thought it was the wind. The four children walked in and they saw an elevator. L'nayah pressed the button. The elevator opened and there were five children's dead bodies. Sophie screamed, running in terror out of the building. There were three girls left. They didn't go in the elevator, they were too creeped out to. There was a scream. Ariarna had gone. There was only blood left. Where was she?

Adriarna Coley (9)
St John's CE Primary School, Failsworth

EVENING EYES

It was a cold evening as the sun disappeared. James and Johnny were investigating the creepy, abandoned Cooper House. It was deadly silent as they walked inside. They pushed open the door and stepped inside. The door slammed behind them. A huge butterfly flew past them, they froze. Everything was still and silent until James shrieked. Johnny looked and saw two huge, green eyes heading towards them. The eyes grew closer. They heard a miaow. It was the cat from Luke's. The door creaked and in came Luke, looking for his cat. James and Johnny left with Luke.

Luke Hulme (10)
St John's CE Primary School, Failsworth

MR FLUFFYPANTS

I'm in the cinema today, watching Killer Clown City. It's really good. It's about one killer clown called Mr Fluffypants. He bites people and they turn into clowns, so there are loads of clowns. Suddenly, a figure is next to me, the figure looks like a clown! Oh no! It walks towards me and I move up a seat. I'm petrified. "Take me," I say.

"What?" he says.

"You're a killer clown," I exclaim.

"No I'm not, I just decided to come here dressed as Mr Fluffypants, that's all."

William Barker (10)
St John's CE Primary School, Failsworth

THE SHORTCUT

Elle and her friends were walking through the woods because they wanted to take a shortcut to Elle's house. Suddenly, they all heard a scream. They stopped, wondering who it was. No one knew who it was, so they went to go and see. They were walking slowly, it felt like a million years passed.

They walked for about ten minutes and then found a funfair. Elle said, "It looks abandoned." They walked even closer and saw that, all of a sudden, the rides started moving. They all got scared and turned around. They all screamed loudly.

Lillie-Mae Nuttall (11)
St John's CE Primary School, Failsworth

THE STORY OF LUCY AND SARAH

There were two girls called Lucy and Sarah. They went to the New Orleans Circus but, what they didn't know was that a clown from the circus had escaped. As they walked through the entrance, the clown popped out from behind the wall. "Hey, do you want to come inside? I'll let you in for free."
Lucy said yes. He took them into a mysterious wood and pulled out a knife. He said, "You'd better run!"
They ran as fast as they could and the clown murdered them. Screams came from the woods as they died...

Emmie Coyne (10)
St John's CE Primary School, Failsworth

THE SCREECH

Ali pointed her trembling head towards the top of the stairs. She slowly walked up the stairs. Ali grabbed the door handle, it made a creaking sound as it opened. The door slammed behind her, she stared around. Everything was covered in dust. Faintly, in the darkness, she could see a skeleton. She backed away and heard a horrible screech. She looked around in horror and swiftly ran downstairs into the living room. But she wasn't in her house...
She later asked a man about her house, but he didn't respond, no one did...

Max Graham (10)
St John's CE Primary School, Failsworth

A MYSTERIOUS DISAPPEARANCE!

I woke up cold, dizzy and scared. I didn't know where I was. The air was dry with a horrible smell. "Hello?" I cried.

There was an eerie silence, but, as I was about to open my mouth... *Bang!* A screw pinged off a poster. I looked at the poster and it said 'Hospital beds' with an arrow. I knew where I was and I wasn't happy about it. I heard a low-pitched voice say, "Come," but it was too overwhelming.

I ran as fast as I could but, unfortunately, I didn't make it out alive!

Megan Eaton (10)
St John's CE Primary School, Failsworth

A SPOOKY, SCARY HALLOWEEN NIGHT

It was a dark, stormy Halloween night and silence filled the room. Suddenly, there was a knock at the door. Terrified, I pulled my duvet over my head - I almost felt like crying! Wait... There it was again! I ran downstairs and cautiously opened the door, tension running through my fingertips. Outside, I saw a bloodthirsty vampire, a hideous, green zombie and a creepy skeleton. I shrieked in fear as they all began to scream, "Trick or treat?"
We all giggled as I scooped some sweets into their cute pumpkin buckets.

Maisy Moe McCaffery (10)
St John's CE Primary School, Failsworth

LOST AND NEVER FOUND

Fred woke up in the Lost and Found cupboard. The wallpaper was peeling and the room looked as though it hadn't been touched in years. As his eyes adjusted to the dark, he saw the door. He got up and left. He was back in the school, except there was nobody around. He looked behind him, the sign said 'Lost and Never Found'. Fred felt confused and scared. The air was pungent, the only thing he could hear was his footsteps. The air tasted odd. He decided to go back. He searched for any secret exits. There were none...

Ben Burgess (9)
St John's CE Primary School, Failsworth

HOLLYWOOD TOWER OF TERROR...

One evening in Hollywood, it was a stormy night; the trees were blowing, the sky was lit with lightning. The Potter family were checking into a hotel. Their room was on the 13th floor. They went to the lift. The lights flashed on and off. The porter said it was because of the storm. The girl pressed the button for their floor. Up they went and, suddenly, the lift began to shudder and shake and then shoot to the ground. The family fell to their deaths. Years later, it was said that their screams could still be heard at night!

Ruby Towers (10)
St John's CE Primary School, Failsworth

THE VISITOR

Jack was in the schoolyard, he had just left school and was on his bike. The sky was dark and he was tired. He had a short journey ahead, but it felt like a century. Then he saw something out of the corner of his eye and... *crash!* Not looking, he had run into a girl in his class. Her name was Violet. "Sorry!" said Jack. Suddenly, the ground started to open and Violet was dragged in. She tried to claw her way out, but the ground closed up. Jack was shocked. He hunted for the beast that did it...

Pawlo Capewell (11)
St John's CE Primary School, Failsworth

THE BASEMENT...

One night, George found a basement in his house and wanted to explore. He went down the creaky steps and found a dark room that smelled like sawdust. He heard a bang coming from the very back of the room. He walked further and further and, every time he looked back, the door was slowly fading away. Suddenly, air brushed through his hair, a piano started playing a song that sounded familiar. Then, cold shaking hands grabbed him around the neck and threw him down to the floor. He blacked out. He was never seen again...

Abbey Farmer (11)
St John's CE Primary School, Failsworth

WAKING MURDERED MILDRED

It was a dark and stormy night in the graveyard. Murdered Mildred awoke from the dead to see a boy holding a book. The boy had used an awakening spell. Mildred couldn't believe she was alive again. Mildred asked the boy if he could wake her family as well. The boy agreed, so they went to the graves where the family were. They woke up Toby, Sofia, Bill, Barbara, Billy, Oscar, Barney and Alex. They had twenty-four hours until they were dead again so they had a huge party and spent time with their living family.

Ferne Bate (9)
St John's CE Primary School, Failsworth

AT THE WRONG PLACE AT THE WRONG TIME

Two explorers entered an abandoned circus, something was lurking in the darkness. Tom and Alice were searching for leftover souvenirs when they were jump-scared by a balloon. But, soon after, they knew they were being followed. They didn't know what it was. All of a sudden, a ghostly shadow swiftly hit Tom and began to chase them until they got two water pistols. The soul was confused, then it got shot by Tom while Alice cowered behind him. The creature melted. It worked out for Alice and Tom in the end.

Dylan Barrett (11)
St John's CE Primary School, Failsworth

NANNIE

I worked nights so I needed a babysitter to mind my two children, it was really hard to find one.

One night, an elderly lady was at the door saying she would mind the children after seeing the advertisement. We had an interview, she seemed great. She started working the next day. The children loved Nannie.

I was talking to my colleague about Nannie and how great she was but, when she heard her name, her face dropped and she said, "I know her. She died in a car crash ten years ago..."

Laila Kesgin (10)
St John's CE Primary School, Failsworth

ONE HALLOWEEN NIGHT

One Halloween night, Lucy and her friends were hanging out in the basement, dressed in their casual clothes, just talking about what was happening in their lives, when suddenly... *bang!* Then there was a scream. They froze. The bang sounded like a gunshot fired next to them! The scream sounded familiar, almost like one of their friends. Lucy and the others looked around and realised that Lily was gone. She was never seen again. People say you can hear Lily's scream every year on Halloween...

Brooke Leigh Flynn (10)
St John's CE Primary School, Failsworth

DEATH IN DUR BURGER

On a dark, scary night, people were in a place called Dur Burger. Lots of people had been eaten by a zombie, a huge zombie! Kiera and Jake were inside, it was haunted! Kiera had a katana and Jake had a power hammer. *Bang!* The zombie broke in with a lot of force. "It's time to fight!" said Kiera.
Clash! Bang! Pow! "The zombie's dying!"
"Yay!"
Then, Kiera sliced the head off the zombie. "He is now defeated!"

Ryan Brandon Osbaldeston (9)
St John's CE Primary School, Failsworth

THE NEW ATTIC

I was all alone at home. *Ding! Ding!* I got a text from my dad, it said 'check out our new attic. Nobody's been in there yet.'
I thought I would check it out. When I first got in there, I thought it was amazing, but then I heard a scary sound. It sounded like a zombie. I was super scared. It was walking towards me... *Oh no!* I even felt a breeze. I was super scared. I saw a little peep of a face. The zombie had hair... It was only my sister, Holly.

Sophie Bradley (10)
St John's CE Primary School, Failsworth

JEFF THE REAPER

One day, I was researching an abandoned village when I heard a blood-piercing scream. A peculiar dead figure ran towards me. I ran the other way, he was known as Jeff the Reaper. I tried to take cover and hide but the building had collapsed on me and I was stuck. I was scared so I shouted for help. I was being watched. Jeff dragged me out of the rubble and ate me!

That was the story of the abandoned village and Jeff the Reaper. If you were me, you'd be scared too!

Nico Wrigley (10)
St John's CE Primary School, Failsworth

THE FACTORY

There was an eerie silence as I fell asleep and woke up in an unknown factory. I heard quiet screams coming closer and closer. I saw a child looking and pointing at a wall. I said, "Hello. What's your name?"
The child looked at me and said in a deep, echoey voice, "Turn around."
The child rudely ignored my question and...
"Boo!"
My sister woke me up. "It's 8.38, you're going to be late for school!"

George-Christopher Brooks (10)
St John's CE Primary School, Failsworth

A SHADOW

At night, Ben was in an abandoned hospital and he was going down a hallway. He went into a room and he heard crying outside. He looked out the window and he found a shadow outside. Ben screamed and ran down the halls, but he dropped his flashlight so it was pitch-black. He stopped and saw blood on the ground. He also saw a shadow, it was a girl. He couldn't move because he was so scared, but he managed to run to the door and escape.

Emily Dunn (9)
St John's CE Primary School, Failsworth

MONSTER IN THE WARDROBE

One stormy night, a little boy called Bob was going to bed after his mum had tucked him in. Then a noise came from the wardrobe. Then he saw some shadows of trees appear on the walls with wind blowing on the branches. There were owl noises too. He shouted for his mum and the noises carried on. Then his mum came in and opened the wardrobe. The noise from the wardrobe was the cat, Buttons!

Lexi Simpson (10)
St John's CE Primary School, Failsworth

THE BASEMENT

One day, a scary basement was discovered by Joshua. He didn't want to go in at first, but then he went into the basement and found a portal. He also found a box full of button-like objects in it. He first checked out the bright blue portal. As he put his hand in the portal, it suddenly disappeared. He set foot in the portal, then both he and the portal disappeared...

Joshua Prescott (10)
St John's CE Primary School, Failsworth

YOUNG WRITERS INFORMATION

We hope you have enjoyed reading this book – and that you will continue to in the coming years.

If you're a young writer who enjoys reading and creative writing, or the parent of an enthusiastic poet or story writer, do visit our website **www.youngwriters.co.uk**. Here you will find free competitions, workshops and games, as well as recommended reads, a poetry glossary and our blog. There's lots to keep budding writers motivated to write!

If you would like to order further copies of this book, or any of our other titles, then please give us a call or order via your online account.

Young Writers
Remus House
Coltsfoot Drive
Peterborough
PE2 9BF
(01733) 890066
info@youngwriters.co.uk

Join in the conversation!
Tips, news, giveaways and much more!

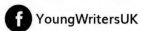 YoungWritersUK    @YoungWritersCW